MOo!

InterRupting
COW

For Alison Stemple,
who must have told me the Interrupting Cow
joke a thousand times
—J. Y.

To Clément, Stéphanie, Melvil et Petit Pois
—J. D.

SIMON SPOTLIGHT
An imprint of Simon & Schuster Children's Publishing Division
1230 Avenue of the Americas, New York, New York 10020
This Simon Spotlight edition August 2020
Text copyright © 2020 by Jane Yolen
Illustrations copyright © 2020 by Joëlle Dreidemy
All rights reserved, including the right of reproduction in whole or in part in any form.
SIMON SPOTLIGHT, READY-TO-READ, and colophon are registered trademarks of
Simon & Schuster, Inc.
For information about special discounts for bulk purchases, please contact Simon & Schuster
Special Sales at 1-866-506-1949 or business@simonandschuster.com.
Manufactured in the United States of America 0720 LAK
10 9 8 7 6 5 4 3 2 1
Library of Congress Control Number 2019921141
ISBN 978-1-5344-5424-8 (hc)
ISBN 978-1-5344-5423-1 (pbk)
ISBN 978-1-5344-5425-5 (eBook)

INTERRUPTING COW

Moo!

by Jane Yolen

illustrated by Joëlle Dreidemy

Ready-to-Read

Simon Spotlight

New York London Toronto Sydney New Delhi

It was morning in the barn.
The cows were enjoying some hay.
Interrupting Cow turned
to her herd mates.
Her name was Daisy.
But as she was always
interrupting (in-ter-RUPT-ing)
everyone, she was called
Interrupting Cow.

"Knock, knock," she said.
"Who's there?" they asked
in their slow way.
They never learned.

"Interrupting Cow," she said.
"Interrupting Cow wh—" they began.
"MOO!" shouted Interrupting Cow.
She fell onto the barn floor
in helpless giggles.

MOO!

Backing out of the barn
and leaving their food behind,
the herd galloped off into the yard.

Interrupting Cow ran after them.
But try as she might,
they would not talk to her
or play with her
or even pay her the slightest bit
of attention.

So Interrupting Cow trotted off
to the duck pond,
where she waded right in.
There the ducks bobbed
and bobbled for weeds,
their feathery back ends
pointing at the sky.

Interrupting Cow waited
until she could count
all of their beaks.
"Knock, knock," she said.
"Who's there?" they quacked back.
They never learned.

"Interrupting Cow," she said.
"Interrupting Cow wh—" they began.
"MOO!" shouted Interrupting Cow.
She fell backward into the water
in helpless laughter.

The ducks swam to the other side
of the pond,
leaving a wiggle of foam
in their wake.
They never looked back.

Interrupting Cow glanced around.
She saw the horses picnicking under
the spreading trees in the meadow.

She trotted over to them.

"Knock, knock," she said.

"Who's there?" they asked
in their proud way.

They never learned.

"Interrupting Cow," she said.

"Interrupting Cow wh—" they began.

"MOO!" shouted Interrupting Cow.

She toppled onto the ground
in helpless snickers.
The horses snorted and sneered,
and galloped away.

She told her joke to the chickens,
who flapped off squawking,
the pigs, who buried their snouts
in the mud,
the goats, who climbed up high
to get away from her,
and the lone donkey,
who went into his shed
and kicked the door shut.

Not a one of them laughed at her joke,
and no one wanted to play.

By now it was late afternoon.
Slowly, Interrupting Cow
walked toward the woods,
where she'd never been before.
She wasn't really afraid.
Just a bit . . . well . . . nervous.
And possibly a little sad.

There, on a branch of a tree
at the edge of the forest,
huddled a strange, dark shape.
She'd never seen anything
like it before.
Interrupting Cow went closer.

"Knock, knock," she called up quietly
to the shape.
The shape opened up big eyes
and stared at her.
"WHOO . . . ," it began.
"Interrupting Cow," she said.
"WHOOOO . . . ," it asked.
"MOO!" shouted Interrupting Cow.

Before she could
fall beneath the tree chuckling,
the dark shape said again,
"WHOOOO . . ."
And Interrupting Cow
interrupted again, "MOO!"

WHOOOO...

WHOOOOO...
MOOOOO!

On and on they went,
interrupting each other
for the rest of the afternoon.
Interrupting Cow had never had
so much fun.

When nighttime came,
the owl flew off on silent wings.
Tired but happy,
Interrupting Cow walked slowly back
to the barn.

She thought she might tell
the other cows
about her long, interesting day,
and about her new friend who liked
to joke as much as she did.
But she was so tired,
she fell fast asleep standing up.
And nobody in the barn
interrupted her very pleasant dreams.